Murder Undone

The Realtor and other stories

by

Paul A. Janson, MD

JM Publishing

ISBN-13: 978-0-9907424-6-3
ISBN-10: 0-9907424-6-6

Published by JM Publishing: May 2018

Author Photography: Sarah McGrath

For more information contact:

Paul Janson
JM Publishing
64 Elm Street
Georgetown, MA 01833

Paul_janson@AOL.com

PaulJanson.com

Dedication

To Mary, my wife and inspiration.

Acknowledgement

I would like to thank so many people for their support and assistance in the preparation of this series of stories. Space will not allow me to thank all of them. It could not have happened without all of you to help.

Contents

Joyce Kilmer wrote:

I think that I shall never see
A poem lovely as a tree

Paul J wrote:

And that is why I'll stop at this
And not go on to finish it.

The words I put upon this page
Will fade and die with passing age.
The page on which they come to be
Was sadly made by killing a tree.

My apologies to Mr. Kilmer and to the tree

The Realtor

A very short story

"It's an old house," the realtor said. "Built to last." She only nodded.

"Not like they build 'em today. Twice as much timber as needed in this one. Last forever, it will."

She nodded again and smiled at him. He'd been a realtor for years and could usually read the buyers easily, especially the ladies. He knew when they liked what he was showing and when they were just looking, but she was different. It was as if she was not really talking about the same thing he was.

"It will need a little fixin' up is all," he tried.

"Yes," she said. "There must be a handyman who could do that. Someone mentioned a man named Luther."

"Well, yeah. Luther could do it, if…" He stopped there. No need to say that Luther drank or that she would be lucky if she got two days' work out of him in a week's time. She just smiled and for a moment, he almost thought she knew about Luther and the drinking. She couldn't know all of it though. Too young to even have been born when Luther was wild. He looked at her again and thought that the girl Luther had killed in that auto crash thirty years ago must have been just about her age. Luther had kept drinking every day since, as if her death had not been important.

"It'll be nice," she said, "when it's finished." With this, she walked up the stairs and opened the front door and he had to move quickly to catch up. It was as if she was the one showing the property.

"Nice entryway." She looked at the ceiling and then at the stairway leading up to the second floor. "Three rooms upstairs," she said.

"Why, yes," he replied. The surprise showed on his face, but she just smiled at him. He hadn't given her the detailed printout on the house. He hadn't had time to make one up.

"Is the furniture being sold with the house?" she asked.

"I think it is. All old furniture, though. You might want something newer."

"I rather like the old-fashioned things," she said.

He looked at her again and thought that she was probably speaking the truth. Her dress was full-length, sweeping the floor as she walked, with her long hair hanging loosely over her shoulders. She looked as if she would have been comfortable in a hippie commune. He thought she matched the furniture as she strolled around the foyer.

Just inside the door was an old mirrored chest, with drawers for gloves and a rack for umbrellas. It was the kind of thing the young people had all liked back thirty or forty years ago when antique furniture was popular.

"There's a nice big room in back you could use for your bedroom," he said, motioning toward the stairs. He expected that she would start up the stairs to look at the room, but instead she turned back and started to walk toward the entry.

"The rooms in front might be more inviting. They will have the sun in the morning I think."

4

He gasped as she passed by him toward the doorway. Not from the words she spoke or the summary decision that the showing was over, but from what he saw, or didn't see, as she walked past the mirror.

His gasp caused her to stop and turn.

"Oh, sorry if I startled you," he said. "But…I…there wasn't, I mean, I didn't see your reflection in that mirror."

He smiled now as embarrassment replaced surprise. "That's silly, of course. There must have been…a reflection, I mean."

"Yes," she said, and walked out the door. It took a few seconds for him to follow.

"So," he began. "What do you—"

"I like it." She looked toward the field next to the house. There was a cemetery there.

"Don't worry about the graveyard." he said. He was relieved to have something to talk about besides the mirror. "There's a highway being built right here. It will make getting out and around easier, and the owners thought that would improve the valuation. That's why they put it on the market. They haven't lived here for years."

"No," she said, still looking at the field where workers were digging.

"Family moved out after their daughter was killed by a drunk driver. That was years ago."

She nodded, but her gaze didn't move from the field.

He cleared his throat. "They have to move that cemetery for the highway."

She said nothing, and the silence seemed to force him to continue. "Strangest thing. They found one of the graves there empty."

"Really?" she said, looking at him. "May I give you a deposit now? It will have to be in cash." She pulled a bundle of hundred-dollar bills from her purse. "I haven't had a chance to get my bank account set up, but this is a thousand dollars. Will that be sufficient?"

"What? Oh, yes, I think so."

His surprise was obvious, but she just handed him the money and turned to look at the house. "I had some jewelry that I no longer needed, and the shop in town was kind enough to buy it from me."

"Well…I don't have a receipt book with me," he managed to say.

"That's all right," she said. "I trust you. Do you think you could have Luther come by tomorrow afternoon to look the place over?"

"Oh, I could bring him by anytime."

She smiled again. "I would rather he came alone. That way he won't be tempted to sugar-coat the estimate just for you."

"Tomorrow's Saturday, but I think Luther will come."

"Yes, Saturday. They won't be working in the graveyard, will they?"

"No. Not on Saturday."

"I'll be here at noon. Can you give me a ride back into town now?"

"Of course. To your motel?"

She just nodded and walked to his car.

***

The next day, she was waiting at noon when Luther arrived. She greeted him and he gave her a looking over. She didn't see any hint of recognition, but hadn't expected that there would be. They looked at the outside and then at the basement.

"A lot to update," Luther ventured, as if he were testing this young lady to see what he could charge. She made no response except to ask him to look at the kitchen.

He was still looking around when she took a pint of whiskey from a drawer and offered him a drink to celebrate. Luther said yes. He didn't notice the white powder in the bottom of the plastic glass as she poured. She sipped hers and refilled his.

When he finished, she thanked him and asked for a written estimate. Then she walked him out to his pickup, thanking him again. He backed onto the lawn and turned, and she walked to the end of the drive. As he drove toward the road, however, she stepped right in front of the pickup and Luther swerved, barely missing her and crashing into a tree beside the drive.

She smiled and sat on the bench next to the drive and watched as Luther stared at her. Maybe there was a hint of recognition now. He fumbled clumsily with the door handle and then his cell phone, to no avail. Finally he slumped back and in a few minutes, he stopped breathing. This was the way she hoped it would end.

She watched until she was sure, and then got the whiskey bottle and her plastic glass, placing them on the floor of the passenger side of the pickup. Luther didn't move.

She took her cell phone from her purse and looked at the unfamiliar device. Finally, she managed to call the realtor.

When she spoke, her calm voice was replaced by one that was more frantic.

"There's been an accident!" she said. "Luther is hurt. Can you come over at once?"

He did, and found Luther dead. Then he called the police. There were two officers; the younger one took down the information.

"Luther just swerved and hit the tree," she said. "I didn't realize how badly he was hurt. I called the realtor. He's the only one I know in town."

"Looks like he'd been drinking," the young officer said. "I'll need a statement from you, Miss..."

"Jones," she said. "Amanda Jones."

The older officer looked up sharply. "That's strange. That was the name of the girl Luther killed in that drunk driving accident thirty years ago."

"That so?" his disinterested partner said.

"She lived in this very house," the older man persisted. A nod was the only response from his partner.

"Can you come by the station tomorrow, Miss Jones, to give that statement?" the young man asked.

"Of course," she replied, but she never did. The realtor was never able to find her to give her a receipt, either, or to sell her the house.

The Priest

A murder undone

Paul Gilligan's life had been one of compromise, or perhaps just surrender. He had never felt as if he were in charge of anything for as far back as his memories extended, so he had chosen a profession where his life had been ordered for him down to the smallest detail. His life's work had been chosen to ensure him of a position of respect with no uncertainty. Paul Gilligan had never been able to "wing it," so he had chosen to become a priest. But life does not always go as we plan it. This morning Paul was greeted by the parish secretary, Grace Imperial. He liked to think of Grace as a source of parish information. Others would have accused Grace of the sin of "gossip."

"Good morning," he said.

"Oh, good morning, Father," Grace replied.

"Are there any messages?" he continued in one of the many rituals that filled his life with certainty, a certainty which might otherwise be called boredom. He did not yet know that today both he and Grace were to be surprised.

"Mrs. Hunter called to say she can't meet with you about the fundraising. Ought to just get off the committee, if you ask me, with all the trouble she's having with that husband of hers."

Her look was one of expectancy, waiting to see how Father would respond to this.

"Oh, I'm sure it will work out. We've still got four months before the carnival anyway," he answered, attempting to sidestep the marital reference. Grace was not about to allow this.

"Father! You're too naive. That man is running around with his secretary, and from what Edith says, he's changing everything he can into cash, and you know what that means. Edith ought to know, being his accountant and all. I'd be surprised if he's here another week. And, it's only three and a half months until the carnival." The note of triumph in Grace Imperial's voice removed all thought of argument from Paul's mind.

"I'll call Mary," was all he could manage to say before retreating into his office.

Once inside, he had time to consider that Grace was most likely right about the future of Carl Hunter. The affair with his secretary was common knowledge, and no one expected his marriage to last much longer. He was talking constantly of a sailing trip to the Caribbean, though never saying when. Paul had himself wondered if this was how he planned to leave. His infidelity had not been brought into any conversation, and Paul thought it never would be. It had not caused any absence from Mass, or for that matter, any diminution in the usual friendly conversation he and Carl carried on about their mutual interest in sailing. He wondered if perhaps he should bring it up, but he dismissed that idea immediately.

Paul found confrontation very difficult. He would no more have been able to tell Carl Hunter that he was destroying a beautiful and holy marriage and placing his immortal soul in jeopardy than he would be able to tell Grace Imperial that she was lacking in Christian charity.

He was beset by doubt as soon as he contemplated it. He always began seeing the reasons behind every action. Life was never black-and-white, always gray. And the grays always looked so much alike to him that he could not bring himself to be judgmental.

He knew that Grace would do anything for Mary Hunter—or for Carl, if she thought it would help. He also knew she had lost her own marriage to an infidelity on the part of her husband; he had run off one night ten years ago (before Paul had arrived at this parish) and had never been heard from again. He knew she had remained bitter since then and had resisted all efforts, including those of her "Church," to bring her any peace. He knew this not from Grace, but from others. He had, in fact, never discussed those long-ago events with her himself. It would have resembled confrontation too much, and led him too close to being judgmental.

Grace's father was another side of this troubled life. He was an alcoholic, and had been drinking heavily during the time when Grace's marriage was coming to an end. He had suffered an accident about that time that required him to be hospitalized, and while hospitalized, had gotten into recovery.

He, in fact, attended Alcoholics Anonymous meetings in the basement of this very church, and had even helped arrange those meetings at the church, but he had never renewed the attendance at Mass required by the faith in which he was raised.

He also had no contact with his daughter, in large part because Grace would not allow it. Paul knew of their relationship because the one night each week that Grace refused to stay late was the night her father would be coming to the AA meeting.

This she had said with considerable force on several occasions. Paul had never discussed her father with Grace either.

Thus, Paul sat contemplating the uncertainties that plagued his structured life when Grace's voice broke into his thoughts. The tone of indignation registered before the words did. "Mr. Hunter would like to speak to you, Father."

Paul's first impulse was to reach for the phone, but he then realized that Carl Hunter was in the church office, standing in the doorway behind Grace. As was often the case, Grace had decided for the priest that he would be able to speak with someone before Paul had an opportunity to consider any alternatives.

"Good morning, Carl," he managed to say with only slight surprise in his voice.

"Good morning, Paul," said Carl. "Just stopped by to drop off a few boating magazines for you."

"Oh, no need to rush over with them." Grace was leaving now with a profound look of triumph on her face. Paul knew he would have to face that look again when Carl left.

There was an awkward silence while the men waited for Grace to excuse herself.

"Had to bring them by; I'm leaving this afternoon to cruise the Caribbean. I wanted to make sure you got them. Had my subscription changed over to your name, too."

"You're leaving so soon?" Paul asked.

"Yes. Wish you were coming along. Good crew is hard to find," Carl replied as he sat down opposite the priest. Paul was glad that Grace was not there to hear this. He knew this was a lie. Carl no more wished to have a priest accompany him than did Paul wish to be there.

Another time, different circumstances, and he would have loved a cruise with a good friend. Some of Paul's happiest moments were when sailing, many of them with Carl. Back in a time when both of them were honest and able to talk about what was on their minds.

"Sailing out with the tide," Carl was saying. "Out of Pigeon's Bay. Around the hook and straight out to sea. Going to be beautiful." And indeed it would be, although Carl's voice was lacking the conviction it might have had. Paul knew that part of the sail well. He'd made it many times before. He knew where the rest of the journey was going, too, although he had never made it himself; he'd seen it all too often. A day sail was one thing, but a cruise such as Carl was embarking on seldom took long to end in misery. Few people can spend the rest of their lives at sea, giving up everything just to keep on sailing. There were more amiable ways to end a marriage than this. What Carl was running from was his life, escaping. But escaping what? Escaping where?

"It will be nice," Paul forced himself to say.

"Yes," said Carl. Uneasiness seemed to be creeping into his voice, now almost palpable in the room. Paul was trying to bring himself to tell Carl what an error he was making, and maybe Carl could feel this coming. He rose abruptly and headed for the door.

"Well, just wanted to make sure you got these," he said, and was gone before Paul had a chance to speak. Paul's head was swirling. What had Carl come for? Not to drop off magazines. This was his goodbye. His mind was as set now as his sails would be set that evening. He was really not ever coming back.

"I'm going downtown for an hour or so," Paul said to Grace as he walked out of the office door. He really did not want to talk to her right then.

He walked for a while past the city's stores, small businesses mostly, leftover from a time when the downtown had been where the city's work was done. When people came to shop or dine or bank: before the "mall." Now what the city had done to the town and country general store was in its turn being done to the city by the mall. Of course now the mall was suffering at the assault of the internet and so it went, full circle. What remained here was an odd collection of those shops already closed and those waiting in ever-increasing decay for the day when they too would be closed.

Interspersed with these were the occasional stores that the fortunes of a changing time had brought to prosperity. Paul was now studying one such prosperous establishment: Al's Guns and Ammo, its sign read. *One man's crime is another man's opportunity,* he thought.

He was thinking of Mary while he watched the people passing the storefront. He could not reach Carl, but Mary would be facing a hard time alone. She must know what everyone else did, though she had said nothing to him and continued her life as usual. In fact, this was the first time she had ever missed an appointment. Yet Grace had been so strong in her words. Maybe Grace knew her feelings went deeper than appearances; that Mary was at the brink, ready to snap. Paul hoped she would be able to move beyond this. Hoped he would be able to help her.

His thoughts were so fixed on her that he was startled when he realized that he was looking at her. She had just emerged from Al's gun shop and was walking quickly down the sidewalk and away from him, clutching her pocketbook.

She was wearing a wig and sunglasses on this cloudy day, but it was she, without a doubt. She had not seen him, had not even looked up from her errand.

A sick feeling came over Paul as he began to realize that Mary might not be prepared to let Carl leave -- that she knew what he was doing, and that she had pretended she was going about her life as usual, all the time preparing . . . she might be planning to stop him with the help that Al had provided. He could not believe what he was thinking, yet what other conclusion could there be?

There were times when the clerical collar was the most valuable part of a priest's equipment: opening doors otherwise closed. This was one such time. Paul walked into Al's shop, not at all sure what he was going to say, but reasonably sure that Al would talk freely to a *man of the cloth*. Most of the people in this neighborhood would identify themselves as Catholic, even if they had not been inside a church since their youth. There was a bond that had been forged in the child that could not be set aside, even in the face of years of neglect from both parties. If the child had not fulfilled the expectations of the Church, neither had the Church lived up to the needs and expectations of the child as he entered into adulthood. Still, these people of this old neighborhood had kept their respect for the Church and its priest, and would consider it an obligation to help him. Paul needed only one look at Al's smiling Irish face to know that he would get all the help Al could offer.

"Good morning, Father," was the greeting that met Paul as he entered the shop.

There was the slightest hint of the brogue still remaining. Paul suspected that most of the time there was none at all, but this was a situation that brought both of them back to a time when the priest was "Father," and the Church was truly sacred and never questioned.

"Good morning. I'm looking for a gift for my brother, and I'm wondering if you could help me," he said.

"Well, I'll surely try. What is it your brother might be wanting?" Al was getting more Irish with every word.

"I'm not really sure. He likes to hunt, you know, deer, I think." Paul was not inventing this part. His brother did hunt, and Paul had never figured out how or why. They just never discussed it.

Al put on a patronizing look. "Not any idea what he would be after then. It's not all that easy, you know. Lots of equipment here, even in a small shop like this, and hunters are pretty fussy, ya know. You could buy him a gift certificate maybe?"

Paul wondered how long it had been since Al had written a gift certificate, or sold anything but a handgun. Again he fell back on the truth: "Well, he lives in Philadelphia. It's sort of a spur-of-the-moment thing. I saw one of my parishioners leaving your shop just now and thought of my brother and the hunting, you know. She just left."

"Ah, you must mean Mrs. Green. She's buying a piece for her husband, she is. And a lucky man he is, too. A hunting rifle, as a matter of fact. For his birthday. Paid cash for it too, so it won't show up on the credit card bill, you know," Al confided with a wink.

Paul was not sure this meant that Al thought she was clever to think of that or that he had not been deceived by this ploy, but Al continued unperturbed. "He can take down a deer at a mile easy, maybe two, if he's as good a shot as his wife is.

"She knows guns all right. Insisted on checking this one out completely before she bought it.

16

"I went with her to the range when she shot it, ya know." He winked at Paul, a knowing wink.

"She's good. Real concerned at how accurate it would be at a distance, ya know. Deer hunting. Knew just what she wanted, too. Probably knows more than me about that rifle. I don't sell many like that. She already has the rifle, just picking up the telescopic sight today. Said it was real important that she have it for this afternoon."

Paul's thoughts were swimming now. He knew now what Mary had in mind, knew exactly, and the deer in the neighborhood had nothing to fear. The rest of his conversation with Al was almost embarrassingly brief. A word or two, and then the: "Thank you, but I must get going." He didn't know what he would do now. What could he do? He did know there was a life about to be lost, maybe two lives.

He knew he couldn't go to the police. What was he going to tell them? They would take too long just talking to him. If he went to Mary and told her what he suspected, she might leave to do what she planned, and he was not sure he could physically stop her. She had a gun, and he did not. She would probably deny it, and then what? She might just kill him as well, and while he might be willing to think about taking that chance to save someone's life, this would not accomplish anything. She might just kill him and then kill Carl.

He knew he had one advantage though. Mary had never been much of a sailor; she didn't even like sailing, much less the more complicated aspects of navigation. Carl had taken great pride in that part of it, and always planned to leave port under sail, with the ebbing tide. This was not at all necessary, as he had an inboard/outboard motor on his sloop that could take him out to sea. But Paul was sure he would be taking himself out with the tide today.

Mary knew that too, but had only a vague idea when the tide would be running out of Pigeons' Bay, and when Carl would be in the channel to catch it, but Paul knew exactly. Mary probably didn't know Carl would want to be in the bay a little before the high tide to catch the retreating ocean at full force.

Paul's interest in sailing was such that he always knew the tide tables, even when no sail was in the plans. He had made this sail so many times with Carl that he knew exactly what time he would be in the channel. He knew exactly when Mary had to act, and she had only a guess at when that would be. With this in mind, he also knew what he must try to do, and he didn't have much time. Speeding would be added to his sins for today.

As he turned down the street toward Mary's home, he could see that her car was still in the driveway. He had arrived in time, but just in time. Mary was coming out the front door as he pulled into the driveway and parked blocking her exit.

"I'm glad I caught you, Mary. Missed you today, and there are a few things I wanted to go over with you. Um . . . could we go inside? Just for a minute." Paul was easing toward the door as he spoke. He had learned long ago how a priest could impose upon people this way.

"Father, I'm really busy. Just on my way out. Could we do this another time please?" Mary was easing toward her car. It was a station wagon, and Paul could see inside. He'd looked as he walked by it and he didn't think there was a rifle in it. He was standing by the front door now, waiting.

"Just a minute," he said.

Mary took on a look of resignation and walked past Paul into the living room and he followed her in. What must be the rifle was lying on the dining room table wrapped in a blanket, ready to go. He had arrived just in time.

"Please be quick, Father," she said. She did not take off her coat. There followed an engagement, almost a battle, with each player trying to outmaneuver the other and always ending in a draw. Paul would ask just one more question, and Mary would supply the answer, saying that she must leave now. Paul had positioned himself near the door so as to psychologically if not physically block her exit. He knew the rifle was in the dining room and that she would be hesitant about picking it up and running out to do that "errand." He was a witness as well as a priest, and she was trying to get away with murder. She would not have gone to all the trouble at Al's if she was thinking of getting caught at this. She was planning to commit murder without anyone suspecting a thing.

He knew he could play this game only so long. The promise that he would be leaving with the next question kept her from leaving without his "permission." He did not think he could physically stop her. She was far more "athletic" than he was, and he did not want to try that anyway. He had another plan. He could not keep her this way indefinitely, but he had an advantage here, too; he had learned to read people, particularly when they were uncomfortable, as they so often were in the presence of a priest. He knew just how long he had to keep Mary here, and he knew how long he could keep her here as well. He was just about at that point now.

"Well, thank you, Mary," he was saying. "I hope I haven't kept you too long." First lying to Al, then speeding, and now another lie. His sins were mounting up fast today. He took his time walking to the car and fastening his seat belt. Another word to Mary and a wave, and then a slow drive down the street. As he turned the corner, he could see her dashing toward the station wagon with the blanket. It was time for him to do some more speeding if he hoped to beat her to the spot. If he had guessed wrong about Carl's plan and he was leaving later than he thought, he wanted to be there in time to try to stop Mary.

By the time he arrived at the bend in the coastal road that wound around Pigeon's Bay, the sun was setting over a calm sea and the colors of the sky were changing with each moment; reflecting across the water in an ever-changing panorama, each color seemingly chosen by the hand of God to testify that the orderliness and beauty of the universe was still His to control. The beauty of the moment was breathtaking to behold, repeated as it was throughout the world as the sun continued its journey, yet different at every one of those points, as if to affirm the versatility of the creation and the Creator alike. Although the spectacle could be explained by the secular science so much a part of modern life, it had yet to be explained why it was beautiful; why a person was moved by its splendor. All the explanations paled when compared to the spectacle itself, just as the creation exceeded the efforts to understand it. The image that now confronted him almost made him forget the events that had brought him to this spot.

In the distance, now almost three miles, he could see a single sailboat heading out toward the open water. He had his binoculars with him and on the stern he could just make out two figures. He knew this would be Carl and his lover.

By now Carl had trimmed the boat to sail on as it was, without the requirement of any intervention by the passengers. Sails and rudder set and with a fair wind, it would continue on this planned course forever.

Well, not forever. Land or a change in the wind would require intervention, but that could be days from now, and if Mary's plan were fulfilled, the passengers would be dead by then. The course they had set would take them away from the course of their friends and fellow sailors alike, into an area less traveled and to where they might never be seen again. The vessel, untended, might drift and eventually sink beneath the waves unnoticed, all their deeds to disappear with them. Even if they were discovered, the events that led to their death might go unsuspected, or at least unproven. No one would know save he and Mary, and of course, the Author of the sunset.

Below him now, on another of the serpentine twists of that coastal road, he could see Mary's car pull to a halt and she jumped out. The rifle was quickly assembled, with only a quick glance toward the sea and the boat now moving away. She was now raising the telescopic sight to her eye. It was too far, wasn't it? The thought flashed into Paul's mind that perhaps it wasn't. Perhaps she could still see them well enough to kill them and leave them on the deck of a pilotless boat sailing out into the sea. The waves crashed up against the rocks and wind blew through trees and grass, but there was no rifle shot.

Mary lowered the sight from her eye and then moved to the very edge of the cliff, as if by moving a few steps closer she could bring them within her reach. The sight was at her eye again—and then it was over. There was nothing she could do now, nothing at all.

He could almost feel the frustration as she hurled the rifle into the sea below. It occurred to Paul that this was probably part of the plan as well. The weapon would never be found down there. It would probably never even have been looked for.

Mary stood watching the sail disappear into the sea and the gathering darkness. Soon they would be beyond her sight, and that would be just as well, thought Paul. He watched too, but he was watching Mary.

He was not sure what she would do now, but was sure that her own death was not a part of the original plan. She would not have gone to such lengths to conceal it if she did not believe she would need to conceal it once it was done.

She could have just shot him where he stood and be done with it easily, but she did not intend to destroy herself with this. Now he wasn't sure what she would do. Finally, Mary got back into her car and drove away. She drove slowly, and he felt that he would have time soon to see her and help her deal with what she had wished to do, and had almost done. Carl was beyond him, sailing away from all help, but to Mary he could give some comfort, and he would.

It was much later than he had thought it would be when he returned to his office. Grace was there waiting for him, and he half-expected to be berated by her for absence, but she was strangely subdued. "Sorry I'm late," he said. "Any messages?"

"There are a couple on your desk," she replied. Then after a moment, she added, "Carl left today."

How did she know? It had been less than two hours ago and yet she already knew. This was one of the mysteries of his life, how Grace always knew. This particular instance was solved, however, when she added that Mary had called. "She said you had been over to see her, about the carnival."

Grace sighed now, no challenge in her tone. "She said she had a couple of thoughts she wanted to discuss with you. When you have time, she said." Grace sounded as if none of this was fooling her in any way.

"Well," he said. "You know my schedule, and how important Mary and the carnival are. Let me know when I have the time." He was not used to surrendering this much authority to Grace, but it felt good to do so. Empowering, even.

He was entering his office now, anticipating that Grace was done with him and would be getting ready to leave for the day, but she followed him into his office. "This reminds me of when my husband left," she said. Her directness should have surprised him, but somehow it didn't.

"Carl reminds me of him too. Thought nobody knew what he was up to, when everybody knew it all along."

"Everyone knew about Carl, didn't they?" he replied. "Even l knew," he added, as if to emphasize the point.

She laughed a little at this, but went on. "My man even packed his suitcase and hid it in the closet, as if I wouldn't notice that all his clothing was missing. But, of course I already knew he and his honey were planning to leave that night. Airline tickets in the mail. That's how they delivered them back then. He never even noticed that I opened them and resealed the envelope. Arrogant bastard!" she added. "I think that bothered me as much as his dumping me."

Paul only nodded.

"I told him I'd kill him if he tried it. Him and that tart both; but he thought he had me fooled. I had a gun you know". Paul was becoming uncomfortable with this conversation.

He didn't think Grace had murdered them and disposed of them somehow, but he didn't know for sure, and he didn't know what she was going to say next.

"I would have too." she said looking out the window.

"What happened?" Paul asked. The content of what she was saying was so astonishing that her language went almost unnoticed. He would only realize later that Grace had never used these words in front of him before.

"It was my damned father again." she said. "That was the night he picked to fall down and break his leg. Drunk again. No one else to help him even get to the hospital. By the time he was taken care of, they were gone. Nobody's ever heard from them again. I guess it's just as well l didn't get there in time to shoot them." she said in an almost casual way.

Paul could only listen.

"Wouldn't have been very good for my son to have a murderer for a mother. I got over it and so did my son."

"That's good," said Paul, in what had to be a contender for the greatest understatement of his life.

"I guess I have my father to thank for it too."

"Did you ever tell him that'?" Paul could not believe he'd said that and Grace apparently couldn't either.

Startled, she replied, "No. No, I haven't."

"Isn't he coming to an AA meeting here tonight? It should be starting in a few minutes."

Grace was coming back to the present now and she was her old self again. "Well, I must be going. I'll see you in the morning, Paul." Paul couldn't recall if she had ever called him by his first name before.

But that was that, or so it seemed. Grace was gone in the few minutes it took him to lock up his desk, but as he walked out onto the sidewalk he saw her standing in front of the church. Her father was just then coming down the street and Paul tried not to notice them, but the look of astonishment on the old man's face said that he had noticed his daughter. As Paul continued down the street he could hear them talking, but he didn't look back. He had other things on his mind, like what he was going to say to Mary when he saw her in the morning. He was sure that Grace would find room in his schedule and he hadn't any idea what he was, and was not going to say to her. Maybe he would just have to wing it.

The Lawyer

I am dying and someone is
trying to kill me

First Chapter

"I am dying, and someone is trying to kill me."

This was my aunt Rose speaking, and while I knew there was a syntax error, I didn't ask what she meant. I had not seen her for maybe three years. We hadn't even spoken on the phone for perhaps three months until yesterday, when she asked me to come immediately. After I fretted about being called back home, I had come to see her. The request, or command, whichever it was, was so unlike her that I had to come. And now here I was, not knowing why I had been summoned or why I had come or what she had meant to say, so I waited.

"I need your help, Frank," she finally said.

"I will if I can," I said. "But I don't know what it is you're talking about."

Aunt Rose had been part of my growing up in this small town, where every one of my family still lived or was buried. Among the buried were my mother and father, Rose's brother.

I had moved to the city, studied law, failed to fulfill the expectations of most people, but in the city only the people who know you, know you have become a failure. In a small town, everyone knows; in fact, more people here probably knew I was a failure than among all four million where I lived. Reason enough not to come back.

"I am dying," she said again. "Cancer. Only six months to live, or so says Doc Cochran. I went to the city and they agreed, only they said six months to live three months ago. I think they're both wrong. I feel like it could be tomorrow."

"I'm sorry," I said, and I was. She had been the matriarch of the family when I was young. Hers was the "family home" where the barbeques were held and Christmas was gathered, and I had enjoyed that part of my time in this town. It was later that I'd decided I had a better future in the city. That I was wrong didn't seem to matter now.

"I know you're sorry, but I don't think everyone can wait," she answered. I waited, waited for more.

"We had a barbeque here last weekend. You would've liked it. Plenty o' beer."

"Don't drink anymore," I said. "Too many lives getting ruined on that account. Mine. Some law firms. My ex-wife. Friend of mine took me to AA and . . . well it's almost a year."

It was almost an apology. I still had trouble admitting to people what was obvious to them. I am an alcoholic.

"Good for you," she said.

"So what about you?"

"Well, we had this barbeque, and someone packed me some extras for later. I haven't been up to much cooking lately. Anyway, Livia had made that awful salad she does, and I figured the chickens wouldn't mind it. Six of 'em were dead in the morning. All spasmed into balls. Poison, I reckon."

"You sure it was the salad? Even I remember Livia's salad and it was bad, but not to kill chickens," I said.

"I only had eight chickens, two now. And I fed one of the ribs to Rufus. He was dead the same way the chickens were. All spasmed up like. I still have some ribs left if you want to try 'em." Before I answered, I remembered Rufus was her dog.

"Some kind o' bad food," I offered. "Sorry about Rufus."

"I'm sorry, too. Rufus was a good ole dog, but I think someone else is sorrier about Rufus. Sorry it wasn't me instead a him. Week before, the brakes went on my car. Jeremy down at the service station. He was jokin' kinda, but a little serious. Asked if anyone would be messin' with the brakes. Punchin' holes in something called the 'master cylinder.' I just laughed. Then, I did—not laughin' now."

She was serious, serious enough to make me nervous. "I think whoever is doing this is going to try again until I'm dead."

"Auntie Rose. Have you talked to the police about this?" I tried to conceal my astonishment. I'm the one from the big city, after all, where people are killed for the most trivial of reasons.

"Aren't you thinkin' here, Frank?" she said.

"Anybody could have messed with the brakes, but only family was at that barbeque. Only one o' my family could have tried to poison me. Clayton's the sheriff, and he's family. He was there. He could be the one."

"Clayton's not smart enough to do anything to a car, but okay, let's say you're right." I was playing for time until I could catch up with what she was saying.

"Who would want to kill you? I mean, everyone knows you're dying, don't they?"

"It's still a small town here. Of course everyone knows. But someone is trying to kill me anyway." She was frustrated. It didn't make sense to her, either.

"Well, okay. Let's say you're right, and someone from the family is trying to kill you. Why?"

The frustration was growing in her. I think she was feeling trapped, and that I couldn't or wouldn't do anything about it. Maybe she'd told someone else and they didn't believe it. "Listen, Frank," she finally said. "I don't have that long to live, but I have some things I want to do. I've got another grandchild I want to see. And Melvin's finally getting straightened out, and I can help set him up in that mini mart store. I don't want to die yet! Not like that. Murdered by someone in my own family, someone in *your* family."

There was a long silence while I still tried to get my mind around this whole thing. Finally I said, "Well, I wasn't at the barbeque."

"That's why I'm talkin' to you, Frank." She was smiling. "I know it wasn't you."

"So, who wants you dead and can't wait another six months?"

"No one, Frank."

"Well, if you're right, someone does, and the only way to stop it is to find out who. So what secrets do you have? As good a place as any to start."

She was exasperated. "There are no secrets here. Everyone here knows everything."

"Not having an affair with someone, are you? Or maybe you know about someone else's affair and haven't gotten around to telling yet."

She was smiling again. "If at my age I were having an affair, I'd take out an ad in the paper. And as for knowing something 'bout someone else, I hear it all; but never first. If I know something worth gettin' killed for, I don't know I know it—and besides, everyone else would know it too."

"Revenge, then?" I offered.

"I don't know of any enemies like that. Besides, it's got to be family."

I thought for a moment. "Well, if it's not a secret or revenge, and it's got to be family, then it's got to be inheritance. Who gets the money, and do they all know who gets it?"

"They all know my will. I divided it up among 'em all. Didn't want to play favorites. Have 'em sayin' I always liked so 'n' so best." She was getting exasperated again, and so was I. "Besides, I'm dying. Can't they wait?"

"Well, if you're sure they all know, then maybe one of them can't wait. How much money is there? Worth killing you for?"

"Frank, really. I'm not that rich. Maybe a million at most."

It was my turn to be surprised. "That's a million *dollars*, right? That include the farm? This place is worth—"

"Well, maybe a half a million there, too," she said. "That's what Milton offered a year ago anyway."

"And that's divided how many ways?"

"Everyone gets an even split. Fifteen all together. That includes the ladies, so it comes to about a hundred thousand apiece."

She didn't seem to realize what she was saying. Where I was living now, people died every day for a whole lot less than that. "That is a shitload of money, Auntie dear. You could get killed ten times over for that."

"I'll thank you to watch your language here, Frank. So, why can't someone wait for it?"

A good question. "Before we jump on that, you haven't led anyone to believe that you're going to give it away to a charity or change the will or anything, have you?"

"No, and I wouldn't. It's family money, and it will go to the family."

"So I guess it does come down to that: who can't wait?"

She didn't answer.

"Let's go at it another way," I said. "Who do you think it might be, and don't try to protect any of them, okay?"

"I don't really know," she sighed. "And that's the truth."

"Well then, let's just bring me up to date on the family, and maybe we can figure this out. Who was at the barbeque, and who could do things to a master cylinder? Run through the list."

"Well, for one thing, the ladies of the city may crawl under cars, but here they don't. Or at least they don't think of doing that." She was probably right. Women don't think about brakes on cars as a way of killing their aunt. Poison, yes.

"So which of my nephews and uncles and male cousins could have, if the ladies are off the list? Why not just tell me about them one by one?" I said.

"Well, a number of them are as old and infirm as I am, and I can't see them under a car, but I'll run through them all and let you decide.

"There's Clayton, the sheriff, and he isn't any different than when you left. Honest, and not very bright."

"Probably not Clayton. Remember that wives can cause husbands to do strange things, so don't eliminate a twosome at murder." Just saying "murder" had made me uneasy, but my aunt went on without a pause.

"Clayton's not smart enough to get married either. Melvin's had a hard time with that broken leg. It never mended and he limps, and drinks, until recently. One day he just stopped, and then got a job at the mini mart. I wanted to help him buy it." She was almost embarrassed by this, it seemed to me.

"Would that use up much of your estate?"

"None," she replied. "Told Melvin I'd help him out, but it'd come out of his share. He thought that would be fine, by the way. Gettin' his share early, I mean."

"Guess he might. Jeremy's family too, and he could do the car. Anyone could do the poison."

"Yes, but Jeremy wasn't at the barbeque. Had to work."

I was glad. Jeremy and I always got along. I would have been disappointed if it had been him. "Okay, who else?"

"Franklin was there, but I've never seen him out of his suit, even at a barbeque. He is also the one that doesn't need the money."

"You sure?" I asked.

"I know what his bank balance is, if that's what you mean. Polly works at the bank." Polly was my cousin, and lived with my aunt when I was last here.

"Is Polly still living with you?"

"Yes, but she was away when the thing with the car happened. I think she's going to marry Clyde Barrow over in Maurytown. Won't do it 'til after I die, she said."

33

"Clyde Barrow? Like Bonnie and Clyde?"

"Yep, only this one's only five foot three and afraid of his own shadow. Polly thinks he's so strong and forceful. They'll be in a world of their own. He was too embarrassed to come to the barbeque. Clinton was there, and he was arguing about something to do with the new bypass. I don't think he thinks about anything that isn't local politics. If we had a mayor, he'd want to be it."

"Any aspirations to go to county or state? A little money could help. Any campaigns revving up that he needs to get into right away?"

"I don't know," she sighed again. "He talked to me about it once. Thought he was going to ask for money, but he didn't. Just bragged about all the connections he had and how he could get things done. I wouldn't be surprised if he didn't want to move into the big time. Happy to be important here. The big fish in the little pond. Ponds don't come much lit'ler than here."

"What about the bypass?" I asked. "Maybe someone might need a little cash to buy up the real estate and make a killing."

"Hell no! It's going to Maurytown. No one wants to come here, and no one here wants 'em to come."

"Now you watch your language, Auntie. What about the twins: Jed and Ned? They never missed food or beer."

"Jed had that car accident, you know. Doesn't seem to know where he is most of the time. Hardly ever drinks. Ned makes up for it though. They both live on Jed's disability. They'll lose that when their inheritance comes in." She seemed a little smug that Ned and Jed would lose that disability income by getting her money. I knew it would only be until they spent it, and that wouldn't take too long.

"Any drugs?"

She was surprised now. "Who? Ned and Jed? This isn't the city, Frank."

"Drugs are everywhere, Auntie dear. What about Uncle Rufus? He's not that old, and he is mean. I remember he killed that dog when I was about fifteen."

"Yes, he could be mean enough, I guess. He's kind to his wife, Alice, and their son; still, I don't know. He's not rich, but I don't think he cares as long as he gets to hunt and fish. I named my dog after him, you know. Make up for the one he killed."

"I didn't know. Would he hold a grudge?"

"About my dog? I don't think he even knew. I wasn't even in his world most of the time."

"He's got a son?"

She smirked. "Bartholomew! Can you believe that? Alice named him. As different from his father as he could be. I heard he passed out at the sight of raw meat. He was here, but if he did anything to hurt anything, I'd drop dead from the surprise. He's gay, you know."

"No, I didn't, but I'm not sure it matters. You sure he wouldn't hurt you?"

"I'm not sure of anything, but he couldn't change a flat tire last time he was here."

"Who else then?"

"Nestor's the only other one. He's still with the fish and game people. Him and Rufus just talk hunting and fishing whenever they see each other. What do you think?"

"I think you'd better be careful and I'd better get busy."

She didn't look at me, and I briefly thought of kissing her forehead but the thought passed.

Second Chapter

I'd driven my own car up from the city, an old wreck of a car, because I had no other choice. Any other transportation would have stretched my budget beyond its limit. That it would cement my credentials as a failure to all who saw me driving it hadn't occurred to me until I climbed into it now. No hope to change that; but it also occurred to me that I could maybe use this evidence of my failure to my advantage. No one would suspect me of being smart enough to interfere, and a murderer would likely think I was here to get my share of the money. I was convinced that was what the murderer had most on his mind. People tended to naturally assume that what they think is important is what everyone else thinks is important.

I needed to eat something now and I needed to think. I also thought I needed to get my mind back into the small town where I had grown up, so I decided to eat at the local ice cream shop creatively named: The Ice Cream Shop. Mary ran it, and she might remember me since we went to high school at the same time. A few years apart, but in this small town and small high school, with small classes, the freshmen were as likely to know the seniors as the other freshmen. They were sometimes even in the same classes. If Mary did not remember, someone there probably would, and my arrival in town would quickly become common knowledge if it wasn't already.

I was pleased to find that Mary remembered me and that she had started serving some food as well. I was also pleased that I was her only customer.

"So what are you doing back in town, Frank?" she asked as I entered the shop. "Here to see your Auntie Rose?"

Jerry, another familiar high school acquaintance, came out from the cooking area that was too small to deserve to be called a kitchen. "Oh hey, Frank," he said. Jerry was blond, and left for California before I left for the city. Rumor was that he had become a surf bum, and his appearance supported that rumor. The blond hair was bushy and in a ponytail, and the tan was better than this town could produce.

"Hey, Jerry. Didn't know you were back home too."

I smiled and turned to Mary,

"Yeah," I said. "Rose asked me to come for a visit." Something about the *karma* in the shop made think that Jerry might have come back to visit Mary. He seemed to be working there, at any rate.

"I heard she was pretty sick," Mary replied. It all seemed so small-town and so logical that she should know. I almost asked if she knew who was trying to kill Auntie Rose.

"Yes," I said.

Jerry let the silence have its allotted time and then asked, "Can we get you some ice cream, or would you rather have a sandwich, Frank?"

"I think a sandwich," I replied. "Maybe a chocolate shake to go with it."

"You got it, man," said Jerry. "This is the tough part now. What sandwich?"

I had to laugh. "Tuna," I said, making it sound more like a suggestion than a request.

Jerry frowned. "Tuna and chocolate? Takin' a chance, but it might work."

This said, Jerry turned and headed back into the prep area to fulfill my wishes, even if they seemed dangerous to him. He also left me and Mary alone to catch up. His instincts must be well-tuned, because that is what I wanted him to do.

"So you know about Auntie Rose?" I said to Mary. I purposely omitted any details, in part to see if she knew any details already.

Mary started on my milk shake as we talked. "Yeah," she said, frowning. "Pretty bad is what I heard."

I decided to extend the test a little more by pretending not to know the details. See how much Mary, and by extension, everyone else, knew about this. "She didn't want to talk about it to me very much," I said. A minor lie for a good cause. "How bad is she?"

Mary was not stupid. She was sizing me up before answering. She either decided I was an honest man, or I was a well-intentioned liar. "I have heard she has terminal cancer. I haven't seen her for a few months, but—how does she look?"

I shrugged. No reason not to be honest. "She looked ill. Chronically ill, but—I don't think she will die very soon."

"No," sighed Mary. "A few more months I heard, but—well, I heard she is not getting any treatment."

"That's what she said," I replied. Mary's scrutiny upped a notch, and I realized I had just contradicted myself. I had said Auntie Rose didn't want to talk to me about her illness, and then said she told me she wasn't getting treated. Not a very good liar for a lawyer.

39

Mary went to law school too, I remembered now, and while she had never practiced, she was better than I was.

She said nothing, and waited to see if I would stumble over my lie. I decided honesty was the best way out of this. "She wanted help with a problem she has," I said. "She didn't go into the details of her illness, but she did say she felt—well, unsafe. She asked me to come because she thought she could trust me because I'm not living here now. She seems to think someone in her own family is . . ."

"Is what?" asked Mary.

Okay, Frank, I thought. *You'd better decide if this lady in front of you is safe to talk to. You've already said too much to back out easily. There's that sandwich coming, too.*

"She seems to think it's her family she has to be afraid of. You're not family, are you, Mary?"

Aunty Rose hadn't mentioned Mary, but I had steered her away from the female relatives. Besides, I wanted Mary to say it herself.

"No kin of hers, Frank. I'm a Burke."

"And Jerry?"

"Is a Wilson. No kin. And I'm getting nervous, Frank. Can I ask you what's going on? Ask you, and expect to get an answer?"

I studied her for a few seconds and then studied the floor. It was a nice floor, white-and-red linoleum, and spotlessly clean. Mary met my standards, too.

"There was a barbeque at Auntie Rose's a week or so ago."

"I heard that. I wasn't there, Frank." The comment was pointed and succinct.

I wondered a bit why she had made it so, but continued anyway. "Auntie Rose's dog died after eating some of the leftovers."

"I heard that too."

My amazement must have shown. I now understood her pointed comment as well.

Mary nodded. "Bert helped Rose bury him. All spasmed up, he said."

I shook my head and Mary smiled. "Rose told Bert not to tell anyone, so Bert—well, he told everyone. Not much fun keeping a secret, is it?"

I had to laugh. "Wouldn't want Bert to miss out on any fun in this boring town. Did he say that her dog was poisoned, and that Rose thought the poison was intended for her?"

"Bert didn't mention that, so I suspect Rose didn't tell him that part or he would have repeated it. Bert is a talker more than a thinker, so he didn't connect those dots."

"Bert didn't," I repeated.

"I did," said Mary.

I smiled at her. "What other dots have you connected, Mary?"

"Rose is dying, maybe a couple months to live. People come to a barbeque, mostly family, and nobody gets sick except her dog. Strange, don't you think?"

"Her chickens died too. After eating some of the leftover salad."

"I didn't hear that. Strange."

I smiled again. "The chickens ate salad and the dog ate ribs. Strange coincidence, I think." Mary smiled back.

Mary's smile expanded a little and she added, "No one got sick at the barbeque, though."

"Not that I heard."

"So . . ." said Mary.

I smiled again. "So, if it was poison, then it was put in the food after the barbeque so—why? So no one except Rose would eat it? And it was put in at least two of the foods that were saved for Rose. Somebody wanted to make sure?"

"Makes sense," replied Mary. "But what doesn't make sense is why. She is going to die in a few months anyway."

"Yes," I said. "Why can't it wait?"

"And where is your sandwich? That's another mystery," said Mary.

She turned and yelled to the back, "Jerry! Where is Frank's sandwich?"

"Almost done!" yelled Jerry.

"Well, bring it out now!! I got a question for you!" said Mary. She turned toward me and added, "Jerry's good at these sorts of things."

I shrugged my apprehension. "Good at sandwiches or attempted murder?"

"Poison," shrugged Mary as Jerry walked out of the prep area with a complete sandwich, chips on the side.

"I toasted the bread. Didn't know if you wanted that. Whole wheat, too. Light on the mayo though. I can add more if you want." He was smiling.

I decided he was good at making sandwiches too, but I wasn't sure about poisonings. I wasn't sure I wanted to know either.

My reticence must have been obvious because Mary answered my unvoiced concerns at once. "Jerry worked as a counselor in a drug rehab back in California."

She paused and then added, "He never used any drugs though. Doesn't even drink alcohol."

I smiled at the small town going around here. "I don't drink or use anymore either. Been, well, a year now."

"I'm glad to hear that," said Mary.

"Yeah," said Jerry. "I smoked weed in high school, but it messes with your brain."

"Yeah," I said. "Everybody was smoking weed in high school."

Mary shook her head. "And I thought I was the only one."

Jerry looked at her and I just shook my head too. I guess this was going according to Mary's script, not mine.

"So what do you know about poisoning people, Jerry?" I asked.

"Not much," he said. "Picked up a little counseling at the rehab is all."

I was beginning to wonder if this was going to help, and Mary was looking annoyed. "What do you think killed Frank's Aunt Rose's dog, Jerry?"

"That the one Bert was talking about, with all the spastic muscles and all?"

"Yes," I said.

Jerry looked pensively about him, but said nothing, and my doubts began to rise again.

"You can be so aggravating, Jerry," Mary finally said. "Say something before the lunch crowd arrives."

"Oh," said Jerry. "Ya see, it depends on—who would have given the poison?"

"If we knew that, Jerry . . ." I began.

"I mean, would it be a doctor or nurse, or just an ordinary person? A lot depends on what the person could get. There are a lot of muscle-stimulating poisons, but only easy to get for someone who is medical. Most ordinary people use a narcotic or sedative."

"Okay," I said.

"No medical types at Rose's barbeque," offered Mary.

"Where would someone get a poison that would cause muscle spasm?" I asked.

Jerry just shrugged. "Easy if you know what you're looking for."

"And what would we be looking for, Jerry?" asked Mary.

"Street drug, you mean?"

I shrugged. My substance of choice was alcohol, and I really didn't get into the street drugs enough to know anything. "Do they sell street 'poisons,' too?"

Jerry shrugged. No condescension. "Any street drug can kill. Most medications can too. It all depends on the dose. Give enough, and you die."

"So . . ." said Mary.

"If it's an ordinary person who's familiar with street drugs, it would likely be strychnine."

"Strychnine!?" I said. "Like rat poison? They sell that on the street? What for?"

Jerry shrugged again. "Used to be in rat poison. Not anymore. Rat poison has some brain swelling stuff now. Pretty gruesome."

"But the dealers sell strychnine, Jerry?" asked Mary. She at least was staying focused, thank God.

"Well, not strychnine itself. They add it to the heroin."

"Which brings us to the next question, complete with expletives: They add it to heroin to what? Kill their clients, for God sakes?"

"They say a little strychnine gives a boost to the heroin. It started showing up in the Netherlands, Amsterdam, in the '70's. Spread from there. I've never used it," said Jerry.

"So," I said, trying to keep up with these two. "How would someone like me get strychnine? Just ask my local dealer?"

"Most dealers aren't going to give you enough to kill someone. Not unless you're real good friends or pay a lot. Dealers don't like to be implicated as an accessory."

"To murder," added Mary.

"Yeah," said Jerry.

"A dealer might be able to get enough strychnine, but he'd have to have a real good reason to give it to you."

"A lot of money?"

"Maybe," said Jerry. "He'd have to know you real well, too. No stranger off the street."

Mary looked pensive and I felt bewildered.

Finally, Mary won. "So the felon here is a good friend of a dealer, like he's buying the heroin, or whatever, on a regular basis, and the dealer has a good reason to want to help him kill his aunt, because like maybe he owes the dealer a shitload of money and the dealer wants, or needs, to get paid, and soon, and the felon is going to inherit that shitload from his aunt if . . . does that sound okay?"

"Could be," Jerry said.

"It sounds like a good guess," I said. "And you sound like a lawyer, Mary."

"Went to law school. Never took the bar exam though."

I smiled. "I went to law school and took the exam. I don't practice anymore though. About the time I decided I wasn't a good lawyer, my law firm figured that out too."

"You two are both pretty smart," said Jerry, beaming.

"How's that?" I asked.

Jerry just smiled. "Most people keep doing things they hate, never realizing they don't have to keep doing them. You and Mary are really smart to know you don't have to do things you hate to do."

He seemed pleased with what he had said, and so was I. "You are smart too, Jerry, smart enough to shut up now before you destroy my new-found confidence in your judgement."

I would have run down the list of possible murderers with them, but just then a customer came in and another car drove up. I didn't recognize any of them.

"I'll see you later, guys," I said, and left to run the list myself.

"You think you can figure it out yourself?" asked Mary.

"Sure. Just going to ask 'em if they're the one who did it and see who says yes. No one ever lies to a lawyer, do they?" I took the shake with me to help fortify me.

Third Chapter

As I drove away, I mulled things over. Aunt Rose had put a number of people on the very unlikely list, and Mary and Jerry, mostly Jerry, had moved some up on the list. While no one was off the list, it looked a little more manageable. Clayton, Franklin, Clinton, Clyde, and Bartholomew were not on Rose's list. Melvin, Rufus, and Nestor might be mean enough, even if not desperate enough. As for someone who could get strychnine easily, well, I would start with Jed and Ned.

It occurred to me as I drove that I might be under a little time urgency here. A failed attempt might spur a more desperate attempt. Finding the murderer might be easier than proving anything, particularly since no one had been murdered yet, and then there was the problem of convincing Rose she needed to turn on one of her own family to save a few months of her life.

First things first; and besides, I thought I knew where Jed and Ned lived. Turned out I was right. It was a rundown address in a rundown section of town. Jed was at the window like he was waiting for me and opened the door for me before I reached it. That was as far as it went though.

No recognition was in his eyes, and no motion to make me welcome or even move aside to let me in. His brother, Ned, came out from the back soon enough, holding a can of brew in his hand.

"That you, Frank?" he said cheerily. "Get ya a beer?"

"No thanks, Ned. I have to drive over to Maurytown this after." I decided on the spur of the moment how I was going to play this, and being a recovering alcoholic was not part of it. Being a drunk would help. "The cops still stake that route out?"

"Better be sober when ya drive it," said Ned with a chuckle. We were bonded now.

"I went by to talk to Auntie Rose," I said. "She didn't look well."

Ned grew a little more reserved now. "Pretty sick."

I didn't think I needed to be subtle here. I thought I could just ask if Ned needed any help with the murder and get a straight answer. "I wanted to find out if—well, I'd heard she was pretty sick and—well, she's got some money that I could sure as hell use right now, but I couldn't find out if I'm in her will, damned bitch."

The bonding was complete. "Yeah, she acts like we should all just wait around to get what's ours. Bitch is right."

Another time would have brought forth other words, but I was on the chase. "So, like, do you know how it gets split up?"

Jed had become bored, or maybe restless, but either way he was wandering off somewhere. Ned smiled. "Everybody gets a share. I seen the will myself. Rose showed it to everybody. Says how much in what bank, or wherever it is, and then her farm to be sold and then everything is split up. Even share to everybody."

He seemed a little disappointed with the next part. "You're on the list, Frankie, same as me and Jed."

I'd gotten used to thinking of Jed and Ned together, so it took a second to remember that they each got a share, twice as much as I would get. I had actually not thought about the fact that I would be an heir at all.

"I could sure use that money," I said, baiting the hook.

"So could I. I got this guy I owe—a lot. He don't want to wait for Rose to die, either. Bastard thinks—"

Ned seemed to realize he was talking too much now and I had heard enough, but I just wanted to zing him one and be sure. "Someone should slip old Rose a little something is what I think."

Ned looked a little surprised and I was afraid I'd pushed a little too hard. I was wrong. "Ya know, Frankie. Rose'd trust you, and well, I got . . ."

I tried to look interested instead of shocked. How stupid could he be?

"We'd better talk again, Frankie. I can't right now. This guy I been—well, he supplies stuff to me and Jed, and we're a little behind. He's comin' over to talk in a few minutes, so, you know. But we should talk later."

I nodded. He'd practically confessed to me.

"Maybe ya ought not to be here when this guy shows up."

"Good thinking," I said. "And Ned, you tell this guy I will make sure he gets what he's owed. I'm on it."

With this I started to leave, but decided to add one more convincing slant. "Maybe I'll take that beer for the road, man."

Ned disappeared quickly and returned with not one but two unopened cans. One for each hand, I guess.

"Thanks, man," I said.

I realized I was laying it on a little thick, but I didn't think Ned needed to be finessed, and I was enjoying it.

The enjoyment was short-lived. As I drove away, I knew that I had no proof, not the kind police would act on. I might be able to convince Rose, but I likely would not be able to convince her to do anything, and finally, I really didn't know what I wanted to convince her to do. Maybe the "guy" coming to visit Ned would be fed up with excuses and eliminate Ned for me, but I didn't think so. Some bodily injuries perhaps, but he wanted money, and a dead Ned wasn't worth a penny.

I felt like I ought to talk to the other people at the barbeque to make sure none of them were suspicious of Ned too. He was so forthcoming to me that I half thought everyone would know.

One of them might just say: *"Oh yeah. Ned's trying to murder Aunt Rose. I saw him put the poison food in her fridge."* Unlikely, but you never know, and having another family member with me when I talked to my dear auntie would be helpful. Alas, it was not to be.

Clayton was first on my list. He was the law enforcement in this town, after all, and it was possible he knew something about drugs being sold and murder being attempted. I found him in his office reading what looked like it could be an official document. I didn't see his lips moving as he read, but that might be because he was not really reading it.

"Afternoon, Clayton," I said.

Clayton nodded, stayed seated, and did not extend his hand in response to my offered handshake. The look on his face said he didn't have any idea who I was.

Go straight at it, I decided. "Aunt Rose's nephew, Frank."

A glimmer of recognition was all the response, and that faded quickly.

After a short pause, I added, "She said she was pretty sick. Asked me to come by and talk to her."

"Heard that," said Clayton.

No sense prolonging this. "She was concerned about some accidents, too. Her car and her dog, Rufus."

"Heard that," Clayton offered again.

"Kind of upset her," I said. "Do you know anything about that?"

"No."

"Well," I said, acknowledging what was obvious, "I'd better get going and let you get back to work. Just thought I'd say hello and mention Aunt Rose's concerns."

"Be around here for a while?" asked Clayton in his longest sentence yet.

"Maybe a few more days."

I waited a few seconds until Clayton nodded and went back to his reading.

Jeremy's garage was next door, and while he wasn't a suspect, he did know about Auntie Rose's car trouble. Besides, I liked Jeremy.

"Hey, Frankie," he said as I walked in. He looked at his greasy hand and I could tell he was wondering if he should offer to shake mine with it. I solved the problem by offering my hand and then slapping his back to prove I was truly glad to shake his hand, grease and all.

"Heard you were back in town," he added, and I wondered who he'd heard this from.

"Yeah. Just for a visit to Auntie Rose." I noticed his smile turning into a frown at the mention of Rose's name.

He paused to look at me carefully before he spoke, but apparently what he saw eased his mind. "She got more'n her share a trouble," he finally said.

51

I nodded. "I heard that. Heard that from her."

He looked first at me, and then beyond me at the car he'd seen me drive up in. "That your car?" he asked.

He knew it was, of course, but this was small-town chatting at its best. "Yes," I said.

"You gonna drive it back to the city?"

"When I leave, yes."

"Maybe you should drop it off here before you leave and let me check it out, ya think? Make sure it can make it back to the city."

"Only about six hours of driving," I replied, but the impact of his words was beginning to sink in before I finished that short sentence.

"Cars have been gettin' trouble visited on 'em round here lately."

It was my turn to study Jeremy carefully. If it had been anyone else, I would have wondered if he were warning me or threatening me. Jeremy was looking after me. "Rose said that, too."

"She heard that from me. I advised her to be careful. I'm advising you, too."

A shiver went down my back at this. Did he really think I was a target? That had not occurred to me.

"Rose said someone messed with her brakes."

"Heard that from me too. That's what it looked like."

"Any idea who could do that?"

He shrugged. "Half the people in this county know how to punch a hole in the master cylinder. The real question is, who'd want to?"

"Any idea on that?"

He shrugged again. "Rose parks her car outside. No garage, so anyone could crawl under it at night and put a hole where it'll leak real slow."

He nodded at me now and then smiled. "Now that dog, Rufus, God rest his poor doggie soul, woulda started barking if someone he didn't know were to be crawlin' around his yard in the middle a the night, don't ya think?"

"I do think," I said.

Jeremy just nodded.

"I'll check in on Rose later," I said as I started to leave. "Want to say hello to my cousin Rufus first."

"Now why didn't ya say so? Him and Nestor are going fishin'. You can probably catch 'em out at Mary's if ya hurry. You remember Mary, don't ya? Runs the ice cream shop."

"Yeah, I remember her. Thanks," I said. I wondered a little why he hadn't heard I'd already visited her.

"You drop that car o' yours by some afternoon and I'll fix it up so's you can get another ten years outta it," said Jeremy. I thought I probably would.

So there they sat as I came in, eating ice cream and talking fishing. "Hey, Rufus, Nestor." They were the only customers.

"Why hey, Frankie. Didn't know you were back in town," said Rufus.

"You're looking good, Frank," added Nestor.

"Thanks," I said. "That your boat out in the parking lot?"

"Sure enough," replied Rufus. "Ain't she a beauty?"

"Sitting there taking up three spaces in my parking lot," scolded Mary as she came over to the counter. "Can I get you something, Frank?"

53

"Ah, Mary. We'll be headin' up to the cabin before the after-dinner crowd gets here."

Mary just shook her head. Her shop might do a good lunchtime business, but dinner was home or a real restaurant. People would come by for ice cream after dinner though, and I was sure the fishermen would be leaving before they arrived.

"Maybe I'll get a small chocolate," I said.

Jerry looked up and said, "That's two chocolate in a row, Frank. Maybe you'd like strawberry instead. It's real good today."

Mary scowled. "All the ice cream at Mary's ice cream shop is always real good, Jerry."

"That's what I said," Jerry smiled. "The strawberry is real good today. Be good tomorrow too, Frank." He then began to scoop, but I couldn't see what flavor.

I turned back to Rufus and Nestor. "I was over talking to Auntie Rose," I said.

Rufus shook his head. "Poor Rose," he said. "Guess she's pretty sick."

"Yeah," said Nestor. "She's like the matriarch of the family. Don't know what it'll be like without her here."

"Heard her dog died, too," added Rufus. "That's sad. He was a good dog. She named him after me."

He was smiling with pride right now. These two either genuinely liked Rose, or they were the best actors in the state. I was betting on sincerity myself. There weren't many good actors in this state.

Whichever it was, the moment passed. Rufus said they'd better be going if the fishing was going to get started before sun-up tomorrow. Nestor agreed, and then looking at Rufus, he nodded toward me.

Rufus looked confused for a minute and then said, "Oh sure, Nestor." He turned to face me and said, "Hey, Frankie. Ya want ta come along? Got plenty of food and stuff. No beer, though. Don't drink no more, ya know."

"His wife won't let him," said Nestor.

"She's right," Rufus replied.

It was undoubtedly a sincere offer and I was flattered. No greater tribute than to be invited on a fishing trip, but . . . "Wish I could, but—maybe next time."

"Yeah, sure," said Rufus. "Take care, Frankie. Come on, Nestor. Thanks, Mary. You too, Jerry."

Five sentences and none longer than three words and they were out the door before Jerry had my ice cream on the counter. It was chocolate with a small scoop of strawberry on top and a smiling Jerry behind it. He was a natural at this, and Mary was lucky to have him. Then again, I thought Jerry was lucky too. I hoped they both realized that.

"I've rounded up the usual suspects," I said, "and I'm heading over to talk to Rose now."

"'The usual suspects.' *Casablanca*, right?" said Jerry.

Mary ignored him. "You know who?" she asked.

"Pretty sure."

"One of the family?"

"Yes," I said.

Mary was cutting to the end game here. The who didn't matter as much as the what to do about it did. "Will you be able to convince Rose?"

"To turn in one of her own family?" I shrugged now. "I'm not sure. Even if he's trying to kill her, I'm not sure. I talked to Jeremy. He pretty much said someone had messed with Rose's car and he thought it was family."

"Interesting," said Mary. "Clinton and Franklin were in here a couple of weeks ago talking about Rose's inheritance, and Clinton said he might paint his house with his share, even though he didn't think it needed it yet."

"Yeah?"

"That's not the interesting part. Franklin just shrugged at it and said: 'Oh, may as well paint the house. A hundred thousand, maybe a little more. Conservatively invested, that would only yield maybe four or five thousand a year at current rates. Not worth that much.'"

"Different world," I said.

"Maybe," Mary replied, "but I don't think Franklin would bother to kill anyone for his share, and I don't think Clinton needs to paint his house enough to kill for it."

"I think Ned needs the money that bad," I said. There was no surprise showing in Mary or Jerry.

"I'm going over to talk to Rose now, but I don't know what to tell her to do. I can't really prove anything, and I'm not sure Rose will take my advice anyway."

I took a bite of the strawberry, put some money on the counter, and waved goodbye.

Final Chapter

The trip to my aunt's farm was not long, and I was driving as slowly as I could to put off the inevitable. I even drove through the one fast food place in town and took a chance on picking up something Rose would like. I got a sample of the menu, planning to offer her first choice and take what she left. She chose first, but made only the weakest of attempts to eat any of it.

While we ate, I explained what I'd found out, and then we came down to the hard part. "So, I'm pretty sure Ned is the one. His brother didn't seem like he knew what was going on around him at all, but I think Ned is going to keep trying." I hadn't mentioned the drug dealer I thought Ned was meeting after I left and that there would likely be some more pressure put on Ned. I didn't think that presenting Auntie with poor Ned being threatened would convince her to turn on him. This was family.

"Ned would kill me to get his inheritance a few months early?" she asked.

"I think he is desperate, very desperate."

"And you think I should, what? Tell Clayton?"

When she said it, it made me realize how unworkable it all might be. "He's going to kill you if he can. He's not going about it in a very smart way, and I want to assure you that if he kills you, I'll do everything I can to make sure he pays."

I hadn't realized until I said it how strongly I felt about this. I also remembered Jeremy saying that cars were being messed with here, and that I had thought he meant that as a warning. If it came to that point, I'd better watch my own back.

"I'll have to think about this, Frank. It's family, and if Ned really needs the money—well, I'm old, and I'm dying, too. What difference would it make?"

My frustration was growing now. She could maybe give Ned his share, maybe Jed, too, but if she did that, would the rest of the family be okay with it? And if she still had most of her estate, would Ned be satisfied, or would he be trying harder to get all that he could? And what if I were wrong and it wasn't Ned?

"Don't think too long, Auntie Rose, and remember that if you are thinking about suicide as a solution, that would likely delay probating the will longer than if you just wait to die." I was trying now to shock her, and while what I had said wasn't exactly true, she didn't know that. I wanted to make sure she wouldn't kill herself tonight. Maybe in the morning I would have a better idea, or maybe Rose would.

I kissed the top of her head and cleaned up the trash and then got into my car to drive away. She looked so alone as I did, and I hated Ned for what he was doing.

It was getting late and I was still a little hungry. I remembered that I'd left nearly a full dish of chocolate ice cream at the shop, and remembered how good the strawberry had tasted. Maybe I could get the chocolate I missed if I offered to help them clean up. Besides, it was the closest thing to sanity I'd seen today. When I got there, Mary looked as if she'd been expecting me.

"How'd it go?" she asked.

"I think I talked her out of committing suicide tonight."

"That's a good start. Want some ice cream?"

"Yeah," I said.

"Chocolate or strawberry, Frank?" called Jerry.

"You decide, Jerry."

Mary looked back at him. "It'll be strawberry. So what happened with Rose?"

"I talked, and she listened, but I'm not sure she heard."

"Heard what, Frank?"

"That Ned wants her dead."

"You're sure it's Ned?"

"I know it's someone, and Ned is at the top of the list."

Mary looked thoughtful for a moment. "What would you do if she did believe you?"

She had me. I couldn't have Ned arrested or any such thing, even if I could prove he put poison in leftover barbeque that killed a dog and some chickens. "Tell her to be careful?" I suggested.

"I think she may be ahead of you, Frank. And"—she shrugged—"what if it isn't Ned?"

Jerry joined us now, depositing three bowls on the counter. He placed strawberry in front of Mary and took the same for himself, and put chocolate in front of me. "Mary likes strawberry too," he said. I had to chuckle.

"So what can I do?" I asked between bites.

Mary shrugged, and Jerry looked pensive beneath his bushy, blond hair. Mary looked at him and said, "It's coming, Frank. Just be patient."

"Well, you know," said Jerry, "I had a friend who was sure his neighbor was trying to steal this Polynesian statue he had. His neighbor was always looking at it, and my friend just thought if he didn't hide it, it would be gone for sure."

"So," said Mary. "What did your friend do?"

Jerry shrugged. "Well, he finally just gave him the statue."

"Gave it to him? Because he was trying to steal it? This isn't making sense."

"That's Jerry. Never makes sense."

Jerry didn't seem to take offense. "No, you see, my friend decided he really didn't like the statue that much and so he gave it to his neighbor. Traded it, I mean, for his surfboard."

"I knew it would be about surfing," said Mary. "It always is with Jerry."

"My friend really liked the board. Still uses it. His neighbor got tired of the Polynesian statue and ended up giving it away."

"Okay, Jerry," I said. "So Aunt Rose should just give Ned the money?"

"Just his share," said Jerry.

Mary smiled. "And then Ned would have his money and have no reason to want Rose dead."

"I thought of that, but I was afraid if Rose kept everyone else's inheritance they'd get pissed, or worse, Ned would up the game and try to get at the rest somehow, and maybe it isn't Ned after all."

Jerry was looking pensive again, but Mary was smiling. "Then Rose should give everyone their share. That's simple enough. Give everyone an equal share of the farm, too."

Jerry was still looking pensive. "Rose should have enough to live on though. She shouldn't feel she's dependent, I mean. That's not good for old people. Messes with their karma."

Mary was looking disgusted, but I was growing happy. "You know, Mary, and Jerry too, she could keep my share. Do some sort of trust so she could spend what she wants, but it could never become part of her estate. It wouldn't belong to her."

Jerry smiled. "You know, Frank, money isn't worth as much as people think it is."

"Yes," said Mary. "A lot of people are fooled by the numbers written on the bills."

Jerry's smile broadened. "Are you going to charge Frank for the ice cream tonight, Mary?"

"Well no, I guess not."

"You see, Frank? All your money can't even buy a dish of ice cream."

Mary shook her head. "You are lucky I love you, Jerry.

"So here we are: two lawyers and a genius," she continued. "My father is a lawyer too, and licensed to boot. He can draw up the papers tomorrow morning."

"That works," I said. "I'll drop by Rose's place and explain it all to her."

"You sure you want to leave your share in a trust for a while, Frank?" Mary asked.

"Yes," I said. "I only wish it could be for a lot longer. She's a sweet lady."

"And you're a sweet guy," said Mary.

"Ah, Mary," I said. "Too bad you love Jerry."

She shrugged. "Yeah, Frank, but I have this real sweet friend, and she has this Polynesian statue she wants to give away."

"Do I have to keep the statue?"

Epilogue

And that's how it worked out. Mary insisted that her father have the paperwork done before noon the next day, Rose signed it, and Mary filed it before she opened the shop. Then we let everyone know it was a done deal, even though it wasn't really done. Everyone, particularly Ned and his dealer, believed it was, and that was what mattered. I personally drove over to his place to tell him, and hung around congratulating him on his good fortune until the dealer came by to verify the rumored settlement. That I was there to reassure him seemed to help. It turned out Ned had a number of other creditors after him too.

Mary treated me to lunch after that, and Polly came by to say that Clyde Barrow had proposed for the fourth time and she had accepted for the first time. He was so surprised that he didn't even have a ring. They were shopping today, not for a ring, just shopping. My guess was that all they were going to buy was a ring.

Clinton came by too, smiling, and asking if I had really left my share in a trust for Rose. When I said yes he grew intensely embarrassed, and finally blurted out that he would make sure Rose was taken care of. Then he added that he would make sure I was treated well too. He left quickly after that, I thought to avoid being seen crying.

Rufus stopped by too, to say the fishing had been good and to offer everyone some of his catch. "Nestor 'n' me got plenty."

When Mary asked if he had heard that Rose's estate had been settled, he looked a little confused. "I guess that means I'll be getting some of her money," he said. He seemed more distressed than pleased. "Don't know what I'll do with it."

"You'll find something," Mary said.

Rufus brightened at once. "You know, my boy, Bart, is talkin' about goin' to college. Imagine that! Maybe I can use some a that money to help pay for it, ya think? If his mother'll let me, I mean."

"She might," said Mary.

"That'd be great. Bart's a real smart boy. You stayin' around for a while, Frankie? Like ya to meet him."

"Yes, Frank," said Mary. "Why don't you stay for a while?"

***

Rose passed away four months later, peacefully, in her bedroom in the farmhouse. She was surrounded by family, all except Ned. He was in a rehab. It turned out his dealer cut him off after he got paid. He said he wasn't a good risk now that the money was gone. I was surprised that Mary really did introduce me to a friend of hers, but she didn't have any Polynesian statues. I don't think anything will come of it, but I'm still hanging around in this small town, doing some work for Mary's dad, and waiting to see what happens next. Jeremy has my car running better than it has in years, but I don't think I'll be driving it back to the city anytime soon. I think Rose would be pleased at how it all turned out.

A further note

For those who might be interested in the discussion of heroin and strychnine that Jerry mentioned in this story I have provided a reference:

Eskes, D. from the Laboratory of the Municipal Police of Amsterdam 117, Amsterdam, Netherlands and Brown, J K. from the School of Pharmacy, University of the Pacific, Stockton, CA, 95207, USA. Published in the United Nations Office of Drugs and Crime (UNODC) Bulletin On Narcotics – 1975, Issue 1-007

https://www.unodc.org/unodc/en/data-and-analysis/bulletin/bulletin_1975-01-01_1_page007.html

This is one of the initial reports and several others followed, including explanations as to why heroin and cocaine are cut with strychnine and what effects are achieved. The pharmaceutical industry tests new medication to obtain information about them, and the street "pharmacists", drug dealers, do the same. The difference is that in the first instance the subjects are recruited and paid, while street dealers use their client as the "Guinea pigs". I have been told this by people I have treated in the emergency department where I worked. These people also verified that strychnine is still used to cut heroin. This is apparently common on the West Coast of the United States and in Asia, particularly Hong Kong where smoking this combination is referred to as "chasing the dragon". I include this note so that you will believe that Jerry is presenting an accurate picture of the drug culture in this country. The truth is often more bizarre than our stories.

Some of these characters are borrowed from a novel I wrote a while ago:

The Ice Cream War: *a mystery of hot fudge and murder*

The Physician

A life undone

She was not one of his patients, but her husband was. She had asked to discuss her husband with him, and he suspected it would be a difficult discussion. Her husband was ill, amyotrophic lateral sclerosis, Lou Gehrig's disease; or more recently, the disease that had finally killed the renowned physicist Steven Hawking. Steven had lived a long time with ALS, much longer than Lou had. Dr. Forrest was prepared to discuss how long she could expect her husband to live. She was younger by at least a decade, and he wondered how she would deal with a prolonged illness.

She had said she would like to go over things completely, and suggested that they meet after he finished his office hours so time would not pressure the conversation. He had willingly agreed. His wife had grown to expect his absence at home, partly because there was not much marriage left to bring him home. She seemed to mind this far less even than he did.

So here he sat with Mrs. Schuster, a desk between them and marriages that were troubled between them as well, but for different reasons, or so he thought.

"It is a terrible disease," he was saying. "No real treatment, and inexorably progressive."

He had used that word, he realized, to impress this woman. She was pretty, and he had appreciated that about her on previous occasions, but this evening she seemed to have taken extra care with her preparation for this meeting. He would enjoy this evening, he thought.

"He will not die soon, then?" she asked.

"There is much better supportive care available these days," said the doctor. He was thinking of Steven Hawking now, who had survived because he had that supportive care around the clock. Expensive care, to be sure, but Dr. Forrest was aware that Mr. Schuster had a great deal of money to spend on that care.

She only nodded.

"We should evaluate his condition and determine what he will need to maximize his life expectancy, and his comfort as well."

"Yes," she said this time.

She moved in her chair, crossing her legs, and Dr. Forrest found himself distracted.

"There is another problem I would like to discuss with you, if you have time," she said, looking first troubled and then embarrassed.

"Well . . . if this will take more time, then perhaps I should let my staff leave. That would remove the time pressure, I mean." He blushed a little, knowing his real reason, and added quickly, "If you feel comfortable."

She was looking at her lap as he spoke and she hesitated a moment. When she raised her gaze she said, "Yes, I think I would be more comfortable that way. Without any . . . it's a rather . . . it's a difficult issue."

He hesitated before picking up his phone and pressing the intercom. "Mrs. Shuster and I are about finished here, Cheryl. I have some computer work to finish, so you may as well go home now."

There was something said on the other end of the conversation. Dr. Forrest still held the phone, but his eyes were running up and down the woman in front of him. She was looking at her lap again and didn't seem to notice, but shifted sideways in her seat, which displayed her to his advantage. When he spoke again, it was almost as if he was coming back and had missed the comments on the other end. "What? No, no. I will be fine."

Again something was said by Cheryl, and again the doctor spoke in reply. "No, Cheryl. I want you to leave now. I will be fine. Now pack up and lock the door on your way out." He waited for no more argument but hung up the phone.

Mrs. Schuster looked up and smiled faintly. "Thank you," she said. "That will make this easier."

She looked at him now with what reminded him of a trapped, abused animal.

"What is it you are . . ."

"Afraid of?" she offered.

"Well, yes." He hadn't thought she was afraid but when she said it, he realized that was what she looked like.

"It's my husband. Peter is abusing me." She looked away and began to cry.

"Abusing you? But he—"

"Has ALS, how can he?" she replied. "You don't know what he is like."

His disbelief was written on his face when the words refused to come from him.

"You don't understand. The police didn't, either. I called them, but they said they didn't see how. A Sergeant Douglas came, but he almost laughed when he saw Peter. He beat me when the useless sergeant was gone."

"But . . ." Dr. Forrest was at a loss now. Her husband, Peter, was limited to his bed and wheelchair. He couldn't—

"He will send the staff away, so it's just the two of us. I have to check on him and when I do—he has his bedroom door fitted with an electric lock, so when I come to his bedroom, I'm locked in.

"He told me if I don't come to the bedroom, he'll report me for abusing him. He has all our money. He says that if he says I abuse him, he'll make sure his lawyers send me to jail for years."

"But surely—"

"He even had a friend of his, a prison guard, come talk to me. To tell me what it would be like in prison. I'd be raped every day, he said."

Dr. Forrest was speechless. Partly from what he had just heard, and partly from what he was seeing.

Mrs. Schuster was taking her blouse off to reveal a sheer bra, her breasts visible through the fabric. She pointed to the bruises on her shoulders. "I'm so embarrassed," she said, "but I have to—to make you believe me."

She turned to show more bruises and whip marks across her back. "Please believe me!"

She was shivering and crying now, and for some strange reason, Dr. Forrest was wondering if insisting that Cheryl leave early was a smart thing to do.

"He has a strap that he ties to my arm so he can pull me over and beat me. Then, he—"

Dr. Forest could listen no more. "But the police can—"

"They can't do a thing. Sergeant Douglas said as much. Peter said if I try to leave, he'll report me to them and they'll arrest me and then . . ."

She was still without her blouse but her composure was back. "I wish he were dead. I wish I knew a man with enough courage to kill the bastard!"

The emotions that were racing over Dr. Forrest were moving so quickly he could hardly keep up with them. When he spoke, it was not what he intended to say. "How would . . ."

She smiled. "I knew you were that courageous man I'm looking for, and I am so grateful that I was right to come to you. I will always be so grateful." She swayed slightly to make it clear what she was talking about.

When he remained silent, she smiled and spoke again. "He has pain medication, and I've been saving it up." The doctor knew he had been refilling the opiates regularly, perhaps too regularly. There could be plenty "saved up."

"I just don't know how to give it to him. I need your help, Doctor. I need it badly." There was another sway, and no effort to retrieve her blouse.

"I know you have a wife," she said. "But we can work things out, I'm sure."

Dr. Forrest was beginning to put this into a plan, and the mention of his wife just added another reason for him to rescue Mrs. Schuster and accept her gratitude.

"When?" he asked.

She smiled and reached for the blouse, bending as she did to offer an even more enticing view. "Tonight, if you can. I don't want to be alone with that man. I think he might kill me. He said he would."

Dr. Forrest was too far into the plan to see any problem or manipulation in what was happening. He did not notice the button from her blouse that was dropped on his office floor, either. She was smiling her gratitude for him to see, and that was all he needed to see. Mr. Schuster was going to die eventually, so it may as well be tonight.

In few minutes, they were driving to her house. They were in his car, at her suggestion. Less obvious, she had said. When it was done, she would tell the police that she found her husband dead and called his doctor. She had already called to send the staff away, saying that she and her husband wanted an evening together after his doctor finished with his visit. There was no one in the house when they arrived except her husband, Peter.

She called Peter to tell him they would be right up and then went to a locked box in her office. When she opened it she said, "They make me keep the opiates locked up." In it was a month's or more worth of morphine. This was more than enough to kill his patient. He filled the syringe he had brought from his office with the lethal dose. He vaguely thought that even if suspicion did arise, Peter Schuster was taking morphine already, and a little more would not show up in an autopsy.

They went to the bedroom where Peter lay in his bed, looking somewhat annoyed. Dr. Forrest knew he could be irascible at times. "Hell of a time to be making house calls, Forrest."

"It's a vaccination you need to get," said his wife. "The flu epidemic."

"Well, let's get it over with," the old man said.

"Yes," said Mrs. Schuster. "We should get this over with as quickly as possible."

Dr. Forrest might have thought about it if he had been given a chance, but he was not afforded any time to think about anything, He placed a rubber tourniquet around the old man's arm, found a vein, and inserted the needle. Mrs. Schuster backed away as he injected the morphine.

He thought perhaps she did so because of some deep revulsion at the murder, or maybe some latent affection she still had. He watched as the breathing slowed and then stopped. He was a doctor, so he felt the pulse, until that too disappeared.

There was a noise from outside the bedroom that finally caused him to turn around and see Mrs. Schuster pointing a small handgun at him.

"Dr. Forrest, you did attack me in your office, tearing a button from my blouse, and then forced me to drive here in your car. You killed my husband, Doctor, and then you tried to rape me. I had to defend myself."

Dr. Forrest began to move toward her, but two shots entered his chest and he crumpled to the floor.

The door opened behind her and she said without looking at all, "You'd better check to make sure he is dead, Sergeant Douglas."

Sergeant Douglas walked to the doctor's lifeless body and did make sure he was dead. He then pulled a handgun in a plastic bag out of his pocket. He careful wrapped the doctor's lifeless hand around it with his gloved hand and then placed it beside the body.

"Looks like the doctor had an unregistered handgun," he said. He then reached over and unzipped the doctor's pants and smiled at her.

"Nice touch," she said. "My blouse should be torn too, don't you think? Can you help me with that too?"

He stood and went over to her and with a swift pull, tore the blouse open. She reached to his face and kissed him as his hand ran up her back. She offered no resistance.

"Thank you, Francis. Your second domestic violence call to this address. Your first report was pretty gruesome. I should thank you for that one too, and the bruises and whip marks I showed the doctor." She looked at her shoulder and said, "I especially enjoyed having you give me these."

He kissed her again, and this time she pulled his hand off her back. "No time now," she said. "Better call for your police backup."

She was still holding her gun in her hand, but dropped it to the floor as he began calling.

"I will always be so grateful to you, Francis," she said.

He smiled broadly and began to speak into his phone, turning away from her as he did.

She smiled and shook her head. "I will always be so grateful, Francis," she whispered. That was the most amazing thing about it all, she thought. Despite all the evidence to the contrary that fool, Sergeant Francis Douglas, actually believed her.

She looked around, vaguely wondering if there were some way to eliminate this fool, Francis, but decided against it right now. She looked at her dead husband and decided she could tolerate Francis for a little while; until she had the money, anyway, but after that . . . .

The Ghost

A story unfinished

If necessity mothers invention, it is desperation that drives job selection. I was desperate that morning when the e-mail announced itself on my cell. "Afraid of Ghosts? Immediate Job Opening. Apply in person." The address was just down the street.

I had an hour before morning coffee with my unemployed friends in the shop across from my apartment, so I headed to the address given in the ad. As I went, I texted John, an equally desperate friend and coffee groupie, to tell him the news. He texted back that he couldn't find the ad, but wished me luck. The sidewalk was crowded and maybe I was distracted, but people seemed to be ignoring me more than usual this morning and I had trouble avoiding them in my haste.

The office was a small store front that I hadn't noticed before, but the door was open and a receptionist was inside at her desk. She looked bored, until she found my name in the list on her clipboard.

A young man was walking past and she stopped him saying, "Mr. Stevens is here."

"Oh, hey," he said. "I'm Frank."

"Paul," I replied, and we shook hands.

"They're expecting you down the street," the receptionist interrupted.

"We will be there in a couple minutes," said Frank. "You're hired, Paul. Come on and I'll explain the job on the way."

It might have been my desperate situation, or maybe it was the enthusiasm that Frank showed, but whatever it was, I said "Great," and we were out the door.

Foot traffic outside was still heavy and still seemed to ignore us, jostling as we trekked in and out. I was a little peeved by this, but Frank didn't even seem to notice.

"Just up here," he said.

"What…?" I began.

"I'll show you when we get there, dude."

By the time I had a chance to speak again, we were standing across the street from my apartment, and I saw myself coming out, reading a newspaper. As we watched, I saw myself walk directly into the path of a taxi.

"What!?" I exclaimed looking at Frank, but by then the taxi had hit the man I was watching, sending him flying to the street. The man was me, and the sound of my head hitting the pavement made it clear that my motionless body was now dead.

The taxi driver was out of his cab as people began to move toward my body. "He just walked right in front of me. Never even looked," the cabbie wailed.

"That's Paul," said the man standing next to me on the sidewalk. I looked at him and recognized my friend John. He looked toward me and then through me to a woman on my other side.

"He said there was an ad … " John began. "Must have been in that newspaper he was reading."

I looked at the dead body lying in the street and then at Frank.

"Now the fun begins," he said.

So that's how I became a ghost, and that's how the fun began.

The Landlord

A Story Untold

I am a writer of sorts, and today I had an experience that I have never had before. I had breakfast with a friend of mine who is a landlord and he told me a story about one of his tenants and his roommates. It was a good story, so good in fact that I can't use it. It would present a situation that would violate the privacy of the people involved and it would be impossible to tell the story without disclosing their identities. If it were not such a good story I might take a chance, but it is good, so good that it might actually be published and so it will remain unwritten I'm afraid. It's a pity, but as they say: sometimes the truth is better than fiction, and sometimes what they say is the truth. The best stories are never told.

About the Author

Paul Janson is a retired emergency medicine physician who has filled his retirement by pursuing his love of literary expression and his love of mysteries, particularly those involving the practice of medicine. He has published six novels, a non-fiction naval history and a dozen children's picture books based on the adoption of his two daughters, all in just four years. He may have to go back to work just to get some rest.

In the meantime he lives with his wife, Mary, of 44 years; two daughters adopted from Ecuador and is helping run a family owned ice cream shop in Groveland, MA. If you're ever in Groveland drop by *Jeff and Marias Ice Cream and Food Shop* and have some ice cream and maybe pick up one of Paul's books too.

Other books by Paul Janson include

Mal Practice a mystery of medicine and murder. Pediatrician Joe Nelson is being sued in a malpractice case involving the death of one of his patients, when he discovers that his patient was murdered. Soon he becomes the next target.

With a Little More Practice: a sequel to Mal Practice. Joe and his friends are in Las Vegas where murder intrudes on their vacation. The victim is a young run away and Joe can't ignore this even when he finds himself at odds with the police.

Scratch a young adult novel of magic and cats. A magical cat saves lives by scratching people and two young sisters are the only ones who seem to realize just how special their cat is.

The Manuscript, a thriller of nuclear terrorism. A literary agent and retired police sergeant uncover a plot to detonate a dirty nuclear bomb when an inmate sends a query letter about a manuscript he has written.

Advance Directive: A sequel to The Manuscript. Someone is killing the patients in the local nursing home to get their inheritance.

The Ice Cream War a mystery of hot fudge and murder. The story of two rival ice cream shops and the body found in one of them. There is murder, humor and a little romance in this story. This is a novel that features Mary and Jerry and their ice cream shop

The Child In Our Hearts. A children's picture book about adoption and based on the belief that all children begin in the heart of their parents regardless of how they come to be in a family and regardless of what kind of family they become a part of. There are several versions of this book for different families, including two mothers and two fathers, and single parents. Some are available in Spanish as well. There is also a version for Assisted Reproductive Technology births.

Battles and Battleships, a narrative history of naval warfare from 1866 to 1905 Paul's first non-fiction work encompassing the development of the battleship a the lessons that can be learned and applied to our current time.

www.ingramcontent.com/pod-product-compliance
Lightning Source LLC
Chambersburg PA
CBHW070525130626
46555CB00003B/1326